Fairy Bread

Becky only wants fairy bread at
her birthday party. But there's so
much left over, and she won't
throw it out. So Becky thinks
of some very strange things
to do with it all.

Tick the Aussie Nibbles you have read!

☐ **FAIRY BREAD**
Ursula Dubosarsky
Illustrated by Mitch Vane

☐ **DUCK SOUNDS**
James Moloney
Illustrated by Stephen Michael King

☐ **SPIDER!**
David Metzenthen
Illustrated by Peter Sheehan

☐ **WHAT DINO SAW**
Victor Kelleher
Illustrated by Tom Jellett

☐ **POP-UP FOX**
Janeen Brian
Illustrated by Beth Norling

☐ **RUFF AND TUMBLE**
Mary Small
Illustrated by Gus Gordon

Visit us at **www.puffin.com.au** to join the
Aussie Nibbles On-line Kids' Club

Aussie Nibbles

Fairy Bread

Ursula Dubosarsky
Illustrated by Mitch Vane

Puffin Books

PUFFIN BOOKS

Published by the Penguin Group
Penguin Group (Australia)
250 Camberwell Road, Camberwell, Victoria 3124, Australia
(a division of Pearson Australia Group Pty Ltd)
Penguin Group (USA) Inc.
375 Hudson Street, New York, New York 10014, USA
Penguin Group (Canada)
10 Alcorn Avenue, Toronto, Ontario, Canada, M4V 3B2
(a division of Pearson Penguin Canada Inc.)
Penguin Books Ltd
80 Strand, London WC2R 0RL, England
Penguin Ireland
25 St Stephen's Green, Dublin 2, Ireland
(a division of Penguin Books Ltd)
Penguin Books India Pvt Ltd
11, Community Centre, Panchsheel Park, New Delhi-110 017, India
Penguin Group (NZ)
Cnr Airborne and Rosedale Roads, Albany, Auckland, New Zealand
(a division of Pearson New Zealand Ltd)
Penguin Books (South Africa) (Pty) Ltd
24 Sturdee Avenue, Rosebank, Johannesburg 2196, South Africa

Penguin Books Ltd, Registered Offices: 80 Strand, London WC2R 0RL, England

First published by Penguin Books Australia, 2001

11 13 15 17 19 18 16 14 12 10

Typeset in New Century School Book by Post Pre-press Group,
Brisbane, Queensland
Printed in Australia by McPherson's Printing Group,
Maryborough, Victoria

Designed by Melissa Fraser, Penguin Design Studio
Series editor: Kay Ronai

National Library of Australia
Cataloguing-in-Publication data:
Dubosarsky, Ursula, 1961– .
Fairy bread.
ISBN 0 14 131175 4.
I. Vane, Mitch. II. Title. (Series: Aussie nibbles).
A823.3

www.puffin.com.au

For dearest Janno and
family, much love, *Urk xxx*

To my beautiful sister Becky. *M.V.*

Chapter One

It was the day before
Becky's birthday party.

'What would you like
to eat at the party?' asked
her mother.

'Um,' said Becky.

'Chips?' said her mother.

'Chocolates? Peanuts?'

'Um,' said Becky.

'Ice-cream?' said her
mother. 'Jelly?'

'Um,' said Becky again.

She was thinking

very hard. Finally she

decided.

'Fairy bread,' said Becky.

'Fairy bread?' said her mother. 'That's it? Fairy bread? Nothing else?'

'Just fairy bread,' replied
Becky.

Delicious!

Chapter Two

The morning of the party,
Becky and her mother were
in the kitchen making fairy
bread. Her baby brother sat
on the floor eating the bits
that fell off the table.

Becky's mother buttered the bread, and Becky sprinkled on all the hundreds and thousands.

Hundreds of thousands
of hundreds and thousands.
Soon there were three big
round plates covered with

fairy bread. They looked

delicious!

Then there were four big

round plates of fairy bread.

Then there were five. And

six. And seven.

After a while, Becky's mother said, 'Is that enough now, Becky?'

'Not yet,' said Becky.

Chapter Three

At three o'clock, Becky and her mother stopped making fairy bread. They had run out of plates.

Anyway, it was time for the party!

The doorbell rang and in
piled her friends one after
another.

'Happy birthday, Becky!'
they shouted and they gave
Becky her presents.

Then they ran around
in circles backwards and
forwards and jumped
on the sofa. They poked
each other in the back

and burst the balloons and
Becky's baby brother cried
and cried.

'Time to eat!' said Becky's
mother.

Everyone stood around
Becky's birthday cake and
sang her happy birthday.
She blew out the candles.

Then they all put their
fingers in and ate up
the cake in gobbles.

No one seemed to notice
the fairy bread.

Chapter Four

'What are we going to do
with all this fairy bread?'
said Becky's mother when
Becky's friends had gone.

The room was filled
with plates and plates

of fairy bread.

'Um,' said Becky.

'I suppose you could have

some in your lunchbox

tomorrow,' said Becky's

mother.

'That's a good idea!'
said Becky, pleased. 'So
could you.'

'Er, yeah,' said Becky's
mother.

Chapter Five

At school next day, Becky
ate several delicious
sandwiches of fairy bread.
And the next day, and the
next day.

Then her mother said,

'There's still so much fairy
bread! What are we going
to do with it?'

'Um,' said Becky.

'I think I'll have to throw it away,' said Becky's mother.

'You can't do that!'

said Becky, shocked. 'You can't throw away my fairy bread!'

'Well, what are we going to do with it?' said Becky's

mother. 'It's getting old and hard. It's stale.'

It was stale. It really wasn't delicious any more.

Even Becky's baby brother
spat it out when she tried
to shove some pieces in
his mouth.

'Yuck!' he said.

'You can't throw it out,' said Becky. 'I'll think of something.'

Chapter Six

She did. Becky had a long long think, sitting on her bed. She thought of lots of interesting things.

She crumbled some up and fed it to her goldfish.

She got a stapler and
stapled some slices together
to make dolls' clothes.

She used a few pieces as

book marks and she stuck

some to the window for

decorations.

Then she got an envelope

and put some slices of fairy
bread inside. She had to
squash them up to fit
them in.

She wrote down her
cousin's Wesley's name and
address on the envelope.

She put a stamp on it and
went down the street and
posted it in the letter box.

'That'll be a nice surprise
for him,' she thought.

Chapter Seven

But there was still so much fairy bread!

'I'll have to throw it away,' said her mother.

'No!' said Becky. 'I'll think of something.'

She thought as hard as
she could. She got a piece
of paper and a texta and
wrote in big letters:

FOR SALE.

FAIRY BREAD.

10 cents. CHEAP.

She took a plate of fairy
bread and went and sat
down on the brick fence at
the front of her house,
holding up the sign.

But nobody came.

Well, one man stopped and looked but he didn't buy anything. He walked away rather quickly.

It started to rain. The
fairy bread got soggy, and
the colours ran.

A cat came and licked
a piece of the fairy bread.

'At least someone liked it,'
thought Becky sadly.

Chapter Eight

'Becky,' said her mother
when she saw Becky with
the plate of wet fairy bread.
'I've got an idea.'

'What?' said Becky.

'Well,' said her mother.

'It's fairy bread, isn't it?'

'Yes,' said Becky.

'So,' said her mother, 'why don't we leave it out tonight for the fairies, and they

might come and take it
away.'

Becky was silent for a
moment. Then she said
sternly, 'But I don't believe

in fairies. And neither
do you.'

'Um,' said Becky's mother.
'But we might be wrong. It's
worth a try. Isn't it?'

Her mother sounded
desperate.

'Hmm,' said Becky.

'Please?' said her mother.

'Oh, all right,' said Becky.

Chapter Nine

So that night, they left
the fairy bread out on
the kitchen table, to see if
the fairies would come and
eat it.

As Becky lay in bed in

the dark, she heard some
funny clanking noises, like
the lid of a rubbish bin.
She sat up.

'Could that be fairies?'
she wondered.

Then the noises stopped.

Becky lay down again

and fell asleep.

Chapter Ten

In the morning, Becky
jumped out of bed and ran
into the kitchen.

All the fairy bread had gone!
They had even washed up
the plates!

Becky stared in disbelief.
She looked at her mother.
She looked at the gleaming
empty plates. She looked at
her mother again, very hard.

'Mum,' said Becky in
a slow voice, 'was it you?'

'Was what me?' said her
mother. She sounded
nervous.

'Did you eat all my
fairy bread?' said Becky.
'Did you?'

'Oh, no,' said Becky's
mother, shaking her head

quickly. She seemed
relieved. 'I didn't, Becky.
Really I didn't. I promise.'

Becky frowned down at the
clean plates again. She didn't

know what to think. If her
mother didn't eat it, what
had happened to it? Could
it have been fairies?

'Hmmmm,' she said to
herself. 'Hmmmmm.'

Her mother sat down on
a chair. She gurgled a bit.

'What's wrong, Mum?'
asked Becky. 'You look
funny.'

'Oh, I'm fine,' said her
mother, with a weak sort of
smile. 'Just tired, you know.'
'You have a lie down,'
said Becky, patting her

mother's arm, kindly. 'I can
make my own lunch today.'

'Oh, all right,' said
Becky's mother. 'Thanks.'

So Becky's mother went

and had a lie down on the
sofa and Becky made her
own lunch.

She couldn't help feeling
glad there was no more
fairy bread.

Peanut-butter sandwiches.

Delicious!

From Ursula Dubosarsky

When I was little (and even now I'm
grown up), a party never seemed
like a real party without fairy
bread. I didn't like eating it that
much, but it had to be there – just
as much as the birthday cake and
candles.

Parties are over so quickly, and the
left-over party food looks so sad – I
never want to throw it away.
I suppose that's how Becky feels.

From Mitch Vane

I have never been to a party where there has been fairy bread left over – probably because I have always been there to eat it all! Poor Becky, I can really understand why she didn't want to waste any of it.

This was a fun story to draw but my hand did get a bit sore drawing all those dots on the fairy bread.

Crystal longs to be a
mermaid. So her mother
makes her a special tail.

Dad saves a scruffy little
dog from being run over.
But whose dog is it?

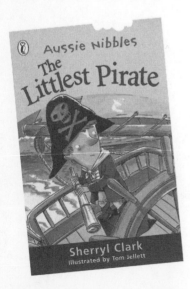

Nicholas Nosh is the littlest
pirate in the world and his
family won't let him go to sea.

Four friends. Best friends fore
Then along came Eartha and
sandpit war . . .